Here It Is!
The Event of the
Century
The Happening of the
Decade
Your Favorite Riddle King
Meets
Your Favorite Arcade
Hero
in a Fun-Packed
Book!
Mike Thaler
Meets
Public Energy #1

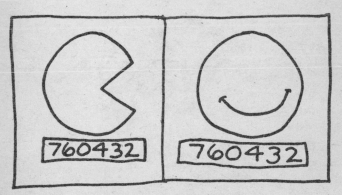

Pac-Man!

Books by Mike Thaler for you to enjoy:

PAWS *Cat Riddles, Cat Jokes and Catoons*
OINKERS AWAY! *Pig Riddles, Cartoons and Jokes*
THE YELLOW BRICK TOAD *Funny Frog Cartoons,*
    Riddles, and Silly Stories
MONSTER KNOCK KNOCKS (with William Cole)

Available from ARCHWAY paperbacks

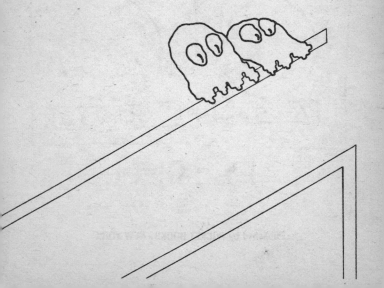

THE PAC-MAN RIDDLE AND JOKE BOOK

BY MIKE THALER
America's Riddle King

AN ARCHWAY PAPERBACK
Published by POCKET BOOKS • NEW YORK

PAC-MAN is a registered trademark of Midway Mfg. Co.

An Archway Paperback published by
POCKET BOOKS, a Simon & Schuster division of
GULF & WESTERN CORPORATION
1230 Avenue of the Americas, New York, N.Y. 10020

ISBN: 0-671-46185-0

First Archway Paperback printing November, 1982

10 9 8 7 6 5 4 3 2 1

AN ARCHWAY PAPERBACK and colophon are
trademarks of Simon & Schuster.

Printed in the U.S.A.

IL 3+

This Book Is Dedicated
in Love and Thanks
to the Young Authors
of Arizona,
Especially Those in the
3rd, 4th and 5th Grades at:

Alma	Senita
Ann Ott	Stanfield
Madison Park	Stevenson
Mercury Mine	Sullivan
Mountain View	Village Vista
Queen Creek	Ward
Rural	and
Sacaton	Washington

Elementary Schools,
for Their Help and Inspiration;
to the Smile Program, Who
Made It All Possible;
and to
Young Authors Everywhere
and the Teachers,
Librarians and Parents
Who Help and Encourage Them
to Create

Pac-Man Favorites

What's Pac-Man's Favorite Restaurant?

And what does he always order there?

A Big Pac

What does he always order in a Chinese restaurant?

Dot suey

In a Greek restaurant?

Shishke-Dots

In a delicatessen?

Dot roast

What's Pac-Man's favorite fruit?

Apridots

What's Ms. Pac-Man's favorite dress pattern?

Polka dots

What's Pac-Man's favorite kind of dog?

A dotshund

What's Pac-Man's favorite video game?

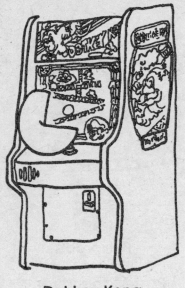

Dot-key Kong

What's Pac-Man's favorite expression?

What's Pac-Man's favorite nursery rhyme?

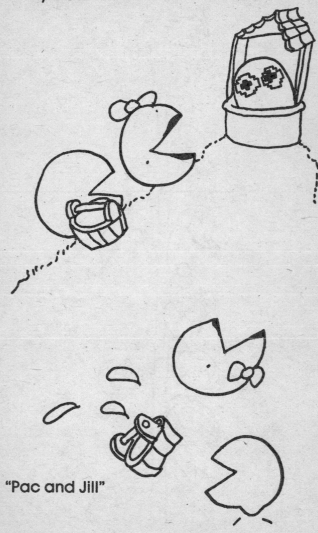

"Pac and Jill"

What's Pac-Man's favorite fairy tale?

"Pac and the Beanstalk"

What's the ghosts' favorite fairy tale?

"Snow White & the Seven Dwarfs":
Inky, Pinky, Blinky, Pokey, Speedy,
Shadow and Dot

What's Pac-Man's favorite astrological sign?

Pac-ces

What is Pac-Man's favorite old car?

A Packard, of course

Who is Pac-Man's favorite race car driver?

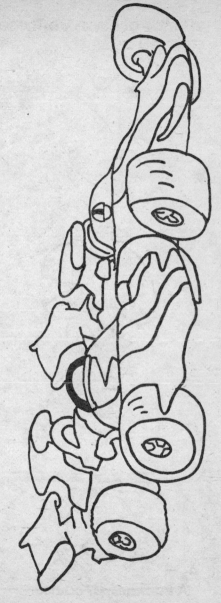

Mario Andotti

What Kinds of Pacs Are These?

1.

2.

3.

4.

5.

NO DEPOSIT

6.

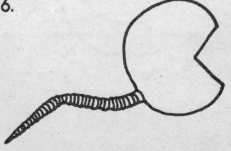

ANSWERS
1. A half Pac
2. An ice Pac
3. A green Pac
4. A back Pac
5. A six Pac
6. A rat Pac

HAVE A NICE DOT

The Adventures of Pac-Man

One day Pac-Man left the video game

and went out on the street, looking for something to eat.

He ate the dots off a lady's dress,

the buttons off a man's coat,

and a little kid's yo-yo.

Then he went to the zoo
to visit the leopard,

to the gym,

and to the movies.

N W PLAYING
A-PAC-A-LIPS
N W

He passed a fruit stand

and ate all the fruit,

was chased by a policeman,

ran into a tunnel,

escaped ...

and lived happily ever after

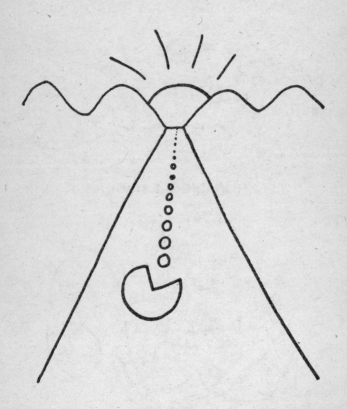

on the open road.

Famous Pac-Men

What Pac-Man was one of the greatest artists of all time?

Leonardo dot Vinci

What Pac-Man discovered Pac-steurization and Pac-cination?

Louis Pac-steur

What Pac-Man is a famous advertising symbol?

Mr. Pac-nut

What Pac-Man is a famous Country and Western singer?

Pac Davis

What Pac-Man was the king of Pac 'n' roll?

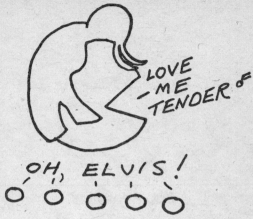

Elvis Pacs-ley

What Pac-Man is the king of opera?

Luciano Pac-arotti

What Pac-Man was the King of England?

Pac Henry VIII

Who was the richest Pac-Man?

John D. Pac-efeller

What Pac-Man is a famous TV detective?

Ko-Pac

What Pac-Man was a famous murderer?

Pac the Ripper

What Pac-Man was a famous frontiersman?

Davy Pac-ett

What Pac-Man is a famous pop singer?

Pac Boone

Who's round and yellow, has a hump and rings bells?

The Hunch-Pac of Notre-Dame

Who's round and yellow and gets a long nose when he tells a lie?

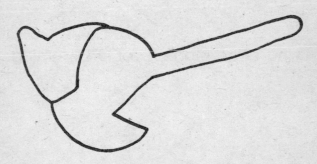

Pac-nocchio

Pac-Man Sports

What's Pac-Man's favorite football team?

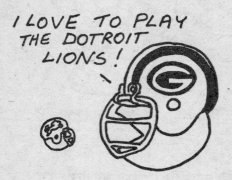

The Green Bay Packers, for sure!

What's Pac-Man's favorite swimming stroke?

The Pac-stroke

What's Pac-Man's favorite target sport?

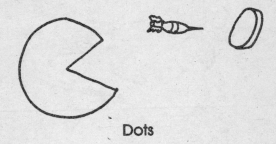

Dots

What's Pac-Man's greatest sporting event?

The Olym-Pacs
Both Pac and field

What's Pac-Man's favorite field event?

The dot-put

What's Pac-Man's favorite court sport?

Pacquetball

What Pac-Man is a great tennis champion?

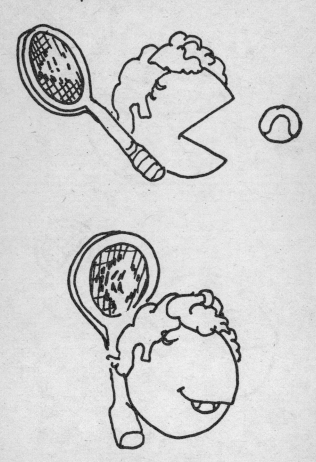

John PacEnroe

What is Pac-Man's favorite table sport?

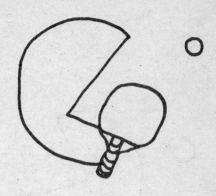

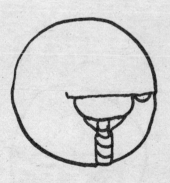

**Pac-Pong,
And he's lousy!**

a lousy golf caddy,

a lousy bowler,

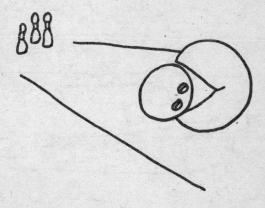

a lousy pool player . . .

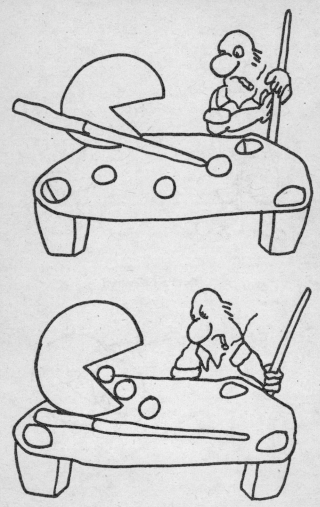

and a lousy yo-yo player

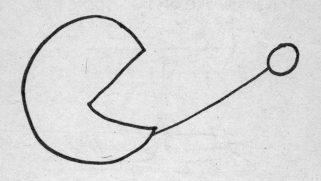

The Birth of Pac-Man

Once in a diner there was a cheesecake and an apple pie.

Everyone ordered apple pie ...

and the cheesecake saw his friend
get smaller...

and smaller...

until . . .

It was gone. Then people started
ordering cheesecake!

And <u>he</u> started getting smaller and smaller.

But the cheesecake decided to fight back.

And he did!

And so was born . . .

Pac-Man.

Pac-Man Riddles

What do you call it when you stick pins in Pac-Man?

Accu-Pac-ture

Where does Pac-Man go for an adjustment?

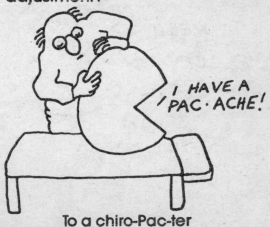

To a chiro-Pac-ter

What does Pac-Man get when he eats too many dots?

In-dot-gestion

What do you call it when Pac-Man breaks out in red spots?

Chicken Pacs

What disease is this?

Small Pacs

What disease is this?

Chicken Pacs

What does Pac-Man clean his teeth with?

Tooth Pacs

What do you call it when Pac-Man improves his bite?

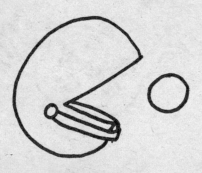

Ortho-doture

How does Pac-Man finish a contract?

He dines on the dotted line

What do you call it when Pac-Man and Ms. Pac-Man take a basket of dots to the country?

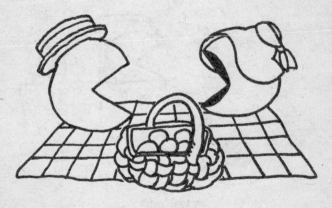

A Pac-nic

What kind of car does Pac-Man drive?

A com-Pac

What kind of truck?

A Dotsun

How far does Pac-Man go on vacation?

He travels from ghost to ghost

Does Pac-Man travel alone?

No, he travels in a Pac

Where do most Pac-Men live?

In Pac-istan

What city has the most Royal Pac-Man Mounties?

WE ALWAYS GET OUR DOT

Winni-Pac, Canadot

What Pac-Men have the most oil?

O-Pac

What's yellow and round and makes Scottish music?

A Pac-bipe

What's Pac-Man's favorite ocean?

The Pac-cific

What's Pac-Man's favorite mountain?

Pac's Peak

What's Pac-Man's favorite climate?

The tro-Pacs

What Pac-Man slept for twenty years?

Pac-Man Winkle

What does every baby Pac-Man use?

A Pac-cifier

What do you call a Pac-Man that won't eat dots?

A Pac-ifist

What Kinds of Pacs Are These?

1.

2.

3.

4.

5.

6.

ANSWERS

1. A Pac-in-the-box
2. A Pac-yderm
3. A Pac-tus
4. A Pac-ademic
5. A Pac-lock
6. A Pac-upine

I GOT THE EATIES FOR MY DOTIES!

Looking Pac

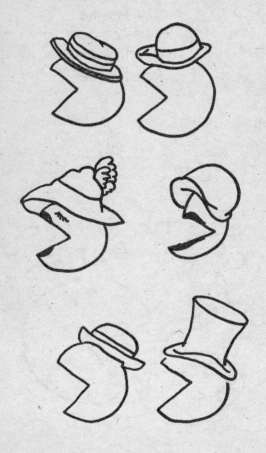

The 1920s

The 1820s

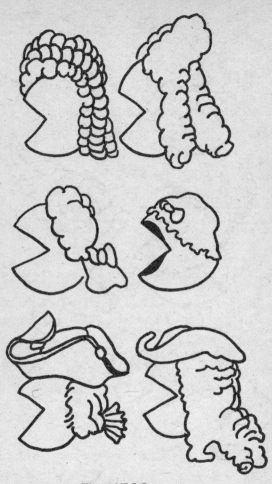

The 1720s

Pac-Man Crosses

What do you get if you cross Pokey
with a cow?

HOWDY

A cow Pokey

What do you get if you cross Pac-Man
with a noodle?

Pac-aroni

With a small dog?

A Pac-ingese

What do you get if you cross Pac-Man with a sweater?

An al-Pac-a sweater

Pac-Man
Knock Knocks

Knock knock.
Who's there?
Pokey.
Pokey who?

A Pokey won't open a good lock.

Knock knock.
Who's there?
Strawberry.
Strawberry who?

Strawberry nice on a hayride!

Knock knock.
Who's there?
Tunnel.
Tunnel who?

A tunnel weigh you down.

Knock knock.
Who's there?
Energizer.
Energizer who?

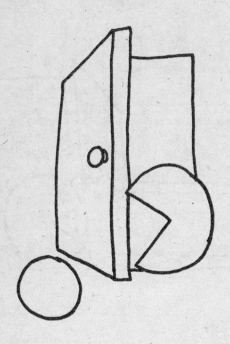

Her hair is gold energizer blue.

Knock knock.
Who's there?
Shadow.
Shadow who?

Shadow–pa you mouth!

Knock knock.
Who's there?
Dots.
Dots who?

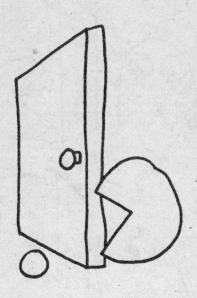

Dots the worst bunch of knock knocks
I ever heard.

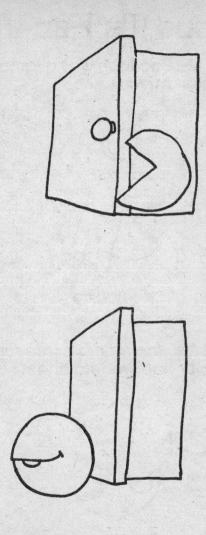

Famous Ms. Pac-Men

What Ms. Pac-Man was a famous Egyptian queen?

Cleo-Pac-tra

What Ms. Pac-Man is a famous Country and Western singer?

Dotty Parton

What Ms. Pac-Man was a famous Indian maiden?

Pac-ahontas

What ghost was a famous Indian maiden?

IM POKEY-HONTAS

What Ms. Pac-Man married a president and a millionaire?

Pac-queline Kennedot Onassis, or Packie O.

What famous Ms. Pac-Man was kidnapped and forced to rob banks?

Pac-tricia Hearst

Dot Jokes

What dot weighs the most?

A hippodotamus

What dots are the most religious?

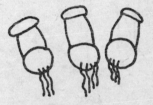

Orthodots

What dot actor smiles the most?

Dot Van Dyke

What is the great dot novel?

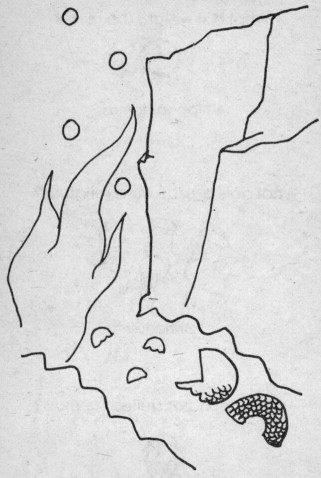

Dottie's *Inferno*

What dot was a great Greek philosopher?

Aridotle

What dot is royalty?

A dotchess

What dot fought windmills?

Dot Quixote

What dot was a great Egyptian
leader?

Anwar Sadot

What dot was a famous movie star?

Dotty Lamour

What famous dot was a robot?

Artoo Dot-too

Pac-Manners

Always visit ghosts when they're blue

Always go through a tunnel first

Always look both ways before crossing an intersection

Always eat everything on your plate

Eat plenty of fruit

And always thank your ghost

Ghost Jokes

What does a ghost say to Pac-Man?

Pac-A-Boo

What are the ghosts' least favorite songs?

The blues

What do ghosts sing when they get eaten?

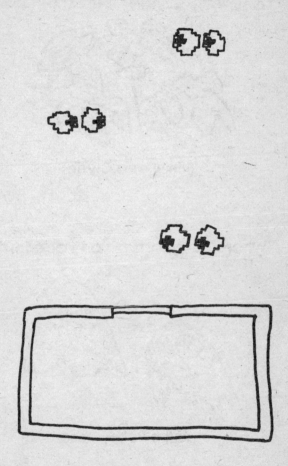

"I Only Have Eyes for You"

What two ghosts were famous bank robbers?

Blinky and Clyde

Where do ghosts go on vacation?

To the Pokey-nose

What sound do you get when Pac-Man's eaten?

A Pac-Moan

Who knows?

The shadow knows!

Pac-Man Goes to the Dentist

Pac-Man Goes to the Doctor

What Kinds of Pacs Are These?

1.

2.

HOWDY

3.

4.

5.

6.

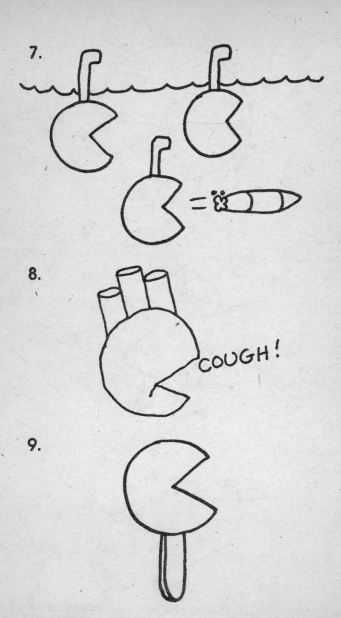

ANSWERS
1. A hockey Pac
2. A cow Pac
3. Piggy-Pac
4. A hippo-Pac-tamus
5. A Pac horse
6. A battery Pac
7. A wolf Pac
8. A cigarette Pac
9. A Pac-Sicle
   or
   A lolli-Pac

Pac-Man Imitating a Shark

Pac-Monsters

Who's round and yellow and sewn together?

Pac-enstein

Who's round and yellow and hairy?

The Wolf-Pac

Who's round and yellow and drinks blood?

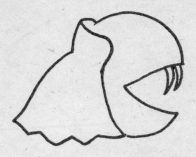

Count Pacula

Who's round and yellow and slimy?

The Creature from the Pac Lagoon

Who's round and yellow and can eat the Goodyear blimp?

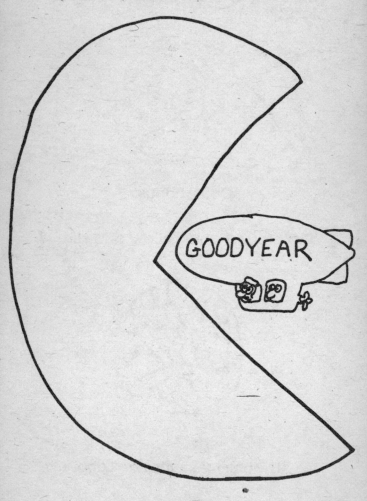

Pac-zilla

Pac-Man Meets Dotzilla

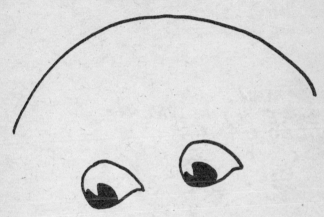

Pac-Man Meets Donkey Kong

Pac-Man Doing the Death Scene from Hamlet

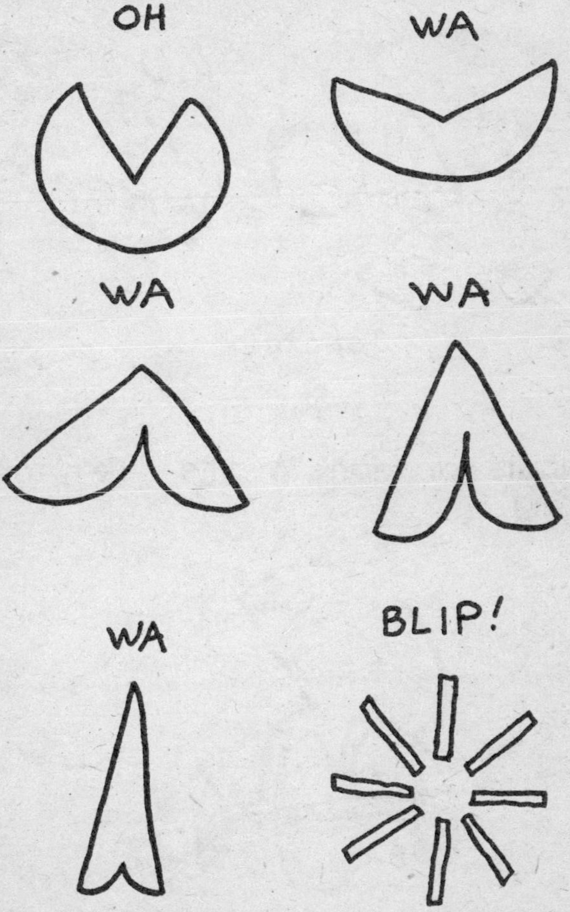

OH

WA

WA

WA

WA

BLIP!

He is a great Pactor!

More Pac-Man Favorites

Who's Pac-Man's favorite rock 'n' roll singer?

Fats Dot-ino

What's Pac-Man's favorite rock 'n' roll song?

"Hit Me with Your Best Dot"

What's Pac-Man's favorite city?

Dot-troit, remember?

What's Pac-Man's favorite game?

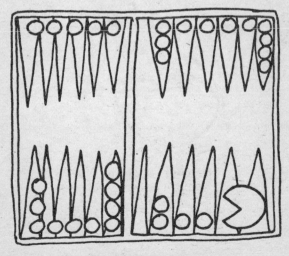

Pac-gammon

What is Pac-Man's almost favorite movie?

Cherry-dots of Fire

What is Pac-Man's favorite George Gershwin tune?

"Rap-speedy in Blue"

Who's Pac-Man's favorite comic?

Dot Rickles

What's Pac-Man's favorite holiday?

St. Pac-trick's Day

What's one of Pac-Man's favorite TV shows?

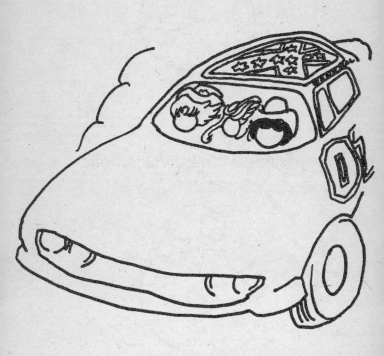

"The Dots of Hazzard"

What's Pac-Man's other favorite TV show?

"Dots Incredible"

Who's Ms. Pac-Man's favorite teen star?

Dot Baio

Who's Pac-Man's favorite movie villain?

Dot Vader

What is Pac-Man's favorite movie?

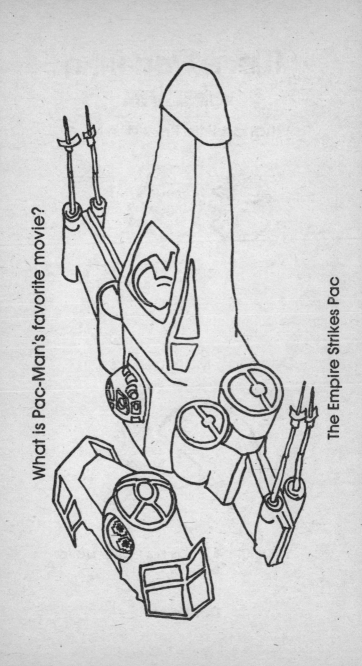

The Empire Strikes Pac

More Pac-Man Riddles

What do little Pac-Men join?

A cub scout Pac

Does Pac-Man love his son?

Yes, but he loves his dotter better

Why did Pac-Man fail writing?

He forgot to eye his dot

Why can't Pac-Man learn Morse code?

Because he always makes a <u>dash</u> for a dot

What's Pac-Man's major problem?

Pac breath

What's Pac-Man's best math skill?

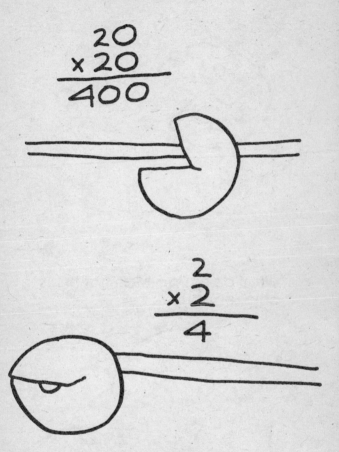

$$\begin{array}{r} 20 \\ \times\,20 \\ \hline 400 \end{array}$$

$$\begin{array}{r} 2 \\ \times\,2 \\ \hline 4 \end{array}$$

Multi-Pac-ation

What's round and yellow and sour?

A dill Packle

What does Pac-Man put in his chicken soup?

Dotzah balls

Where's the best place to keep dots?

In your back Pac-et

What does a dot ride in?

A Paxi-cab

What do you call it when Pac-Man plays a trick on someone?

A Pac-tickle joke

What do you call Pac-Man pimples?

Pac-ne

Who's round and yellow and lives in the sky?

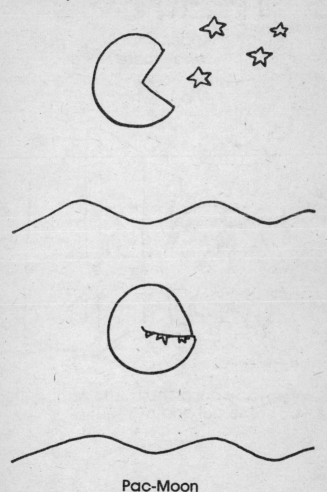

Pac-Moon

More Pac-Man
Knock Knocks

Knock knock.
Who's there?
Video.
Video who?

Video lady out of the house, why don't you come out and play?

Knock knock.
Who's there?
Ms. Pac-Man
Ms. Pac-Man who?

I **Ms. Pac-Man** a lot when he goes away.

Knock knock.
Who's there?

Joy stick.
Joy stick who?

Joy Stick around too long and a ghost'll get ya!

Pac-Man
Super Heroes

What Pac-Man is a famous cat?

The Pac Panther

A famous crime fighter?

Pat-Man

A famous detective?

Dot Tracy

A famous flying hero?

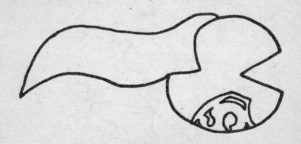

Pac-super-man

A famous cartoon bird?

Woody Wood-Pac-ker

And a famous cartoon pig?

Packy Pig

The Author
A Self-Pactrait

ABOUT THE AUTHOR

MIKE THALER, America's Riddle King and the creator of Letterman on TV's "Electric Company," has met Pac-Man and won a new high score in humor. The author of more than eighty books for children, ranging from original riddle and joke books to fables and picture books, does it again! *The Saturday Review* has called him "one of the most creative people in children's books today."

Mike is also a sculptor, a songwriter and an educator who has created a bookmaking process for groups of children and their teachers. He is a sought-after speaker who enjoys giving many workshops and programs for children and adults across the country.

Above all, he believes in creativity—in himself and in others. As Mike explains it: "That is my life and my work."